To King Romy. Long may she reign!
—𝔐. ℭ.

a Feiwel and Friends book
An imprint of Macmillan Publishing Group, LLC
175 Fifth Avenue, New York, NY 10010

Our books may be purchased in bulk for promotional, educational, or business use.
Please contact your local bookseller or the Macmillan Corporate and Premium Sales Department
at (800) 221-7945 ext. 5442 or by e-mail at MacmillanSpecialMarkets@macmillan.com.

Library of Congress Cataloging-in-Publication Data is available.

ISBN 978-1-250-04749-6 (hardcover)

The artwork for this book was created using pen and ink, watercolor, and whatever colored
pencils and markers Matthew Cordell could find from his kids' stash of art supplies.

Feiwel and Friends logo designed by Filomena Tuosto

First edition, 2018

1 3 5 7 9 10 8 6 4 2

mackids.com

King Alice

Matthew Cordell

Feiwel and Friends • New York

scratch
scritch

"Y-a-a-a-a-w-n . . . Morning, Alice," said Dad.

"No! **KING** Alice! The First!" shouted Alice.

"You mean . . . Queen?" asked Dad.

"No! **KING**!"

"Ummm . . . King," Dad said.

"Idea!" said Alice. "Let's make . . .
super-sparkly strawberry muffins again!"
"Ummm . . . ," Dad said. "How about something else?"

"Idea!" said Alice. "Let's make . . .
you look super-duper pretty again!"
"Ummm . . . ," Dad said. "How about something else?"

"Idea!" said Alice. "Let's make . . . a . . . book!"

"Ummm . . . A book?" asked Dad.

"A book about what?" asked Mom.

"A book about King Alice the First! A-a-a-n-d . . .
the royal brave knights!"

"King Alice the First and the royal brave
knights having breakfast," said Mom.

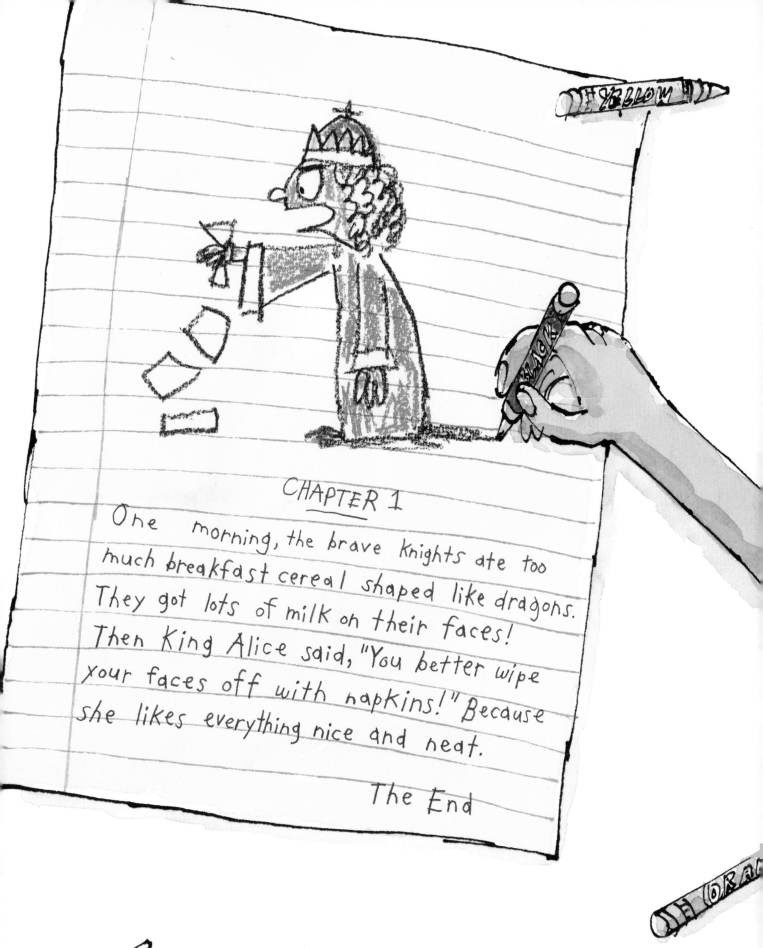

CHAPTER 1

One morning, the brave knights ate too much breakfast cereal shaped like dragons. They got lots of milk on their faces! Then King Alice said, "You better wipe your faces off with napkins!" Because she likes everything nice and neat.

The End

"Ummm . . . ," Dad said.

"Rather short, isn't it?" asked Mom. "Anything else?"

"Hmm . . . ," thought Alice. "Idea . . . !"

"King Alice the First and the royal brave knights' PRINCESS TEA PARTY!"

(NOT The End)

CHAPTER 2

Then it was time for a snack, so King Alice and the Knights went to the princess tea party and had chocolate chip cookies and chamomile tea. King Alice yelled, "This is some delicious tea!"

"Well, okay, yes, but you have cookie all over your face," said Princess Peanut.

"HA HA, oh what good cookies," said the Knights.

Knight Baby burped and said, "Excuse me."

"Okay, I'm bored now.

I don't want to do the book anymore," Alice decided.

"But . . . ," said Dad.

"Let's play with my Kitty Babies."

"Brush, brush, brush, Kitty Baby.
Brush, Kitty Baby. Brush."

"IDEA!"

"CHAPTER 5!" Alice announced.
"What happened to chapters 3 and 4 . . . ?"
Dad wondered pointlessly.

CHAPTER 5

Then the pirates came in their big pirate car! Captain Bellyfish walked around and said, "I'm the toughest pirate on Earth!"

And the little pirate said, "No more cookies?! Then you will all eat fish, Knight Princesses, and I won't say please! Walk the plank!"

But King Alice tooted and it made everyone laugh. They all decided to be friends instead.

Toot

Lunch time!

"Can't I just watch TV now?
I'm too tired to *create*," Alice yawned.

"I'm so, so, so, so, so sorry I bonked you with my unicorn, Daddy. You are funny and nice and you draw good and smell good and are neat and nice and will you still play with me now, Daddy?"

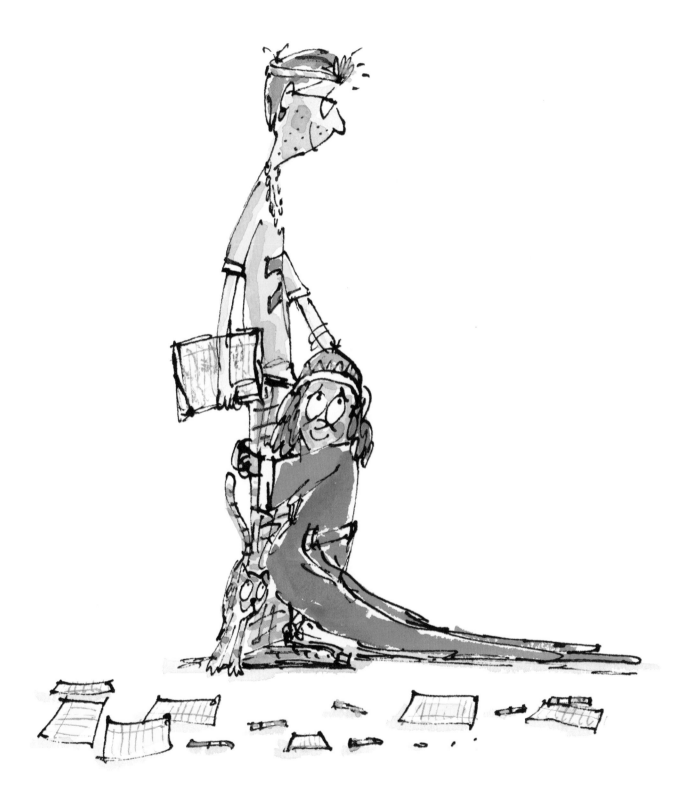

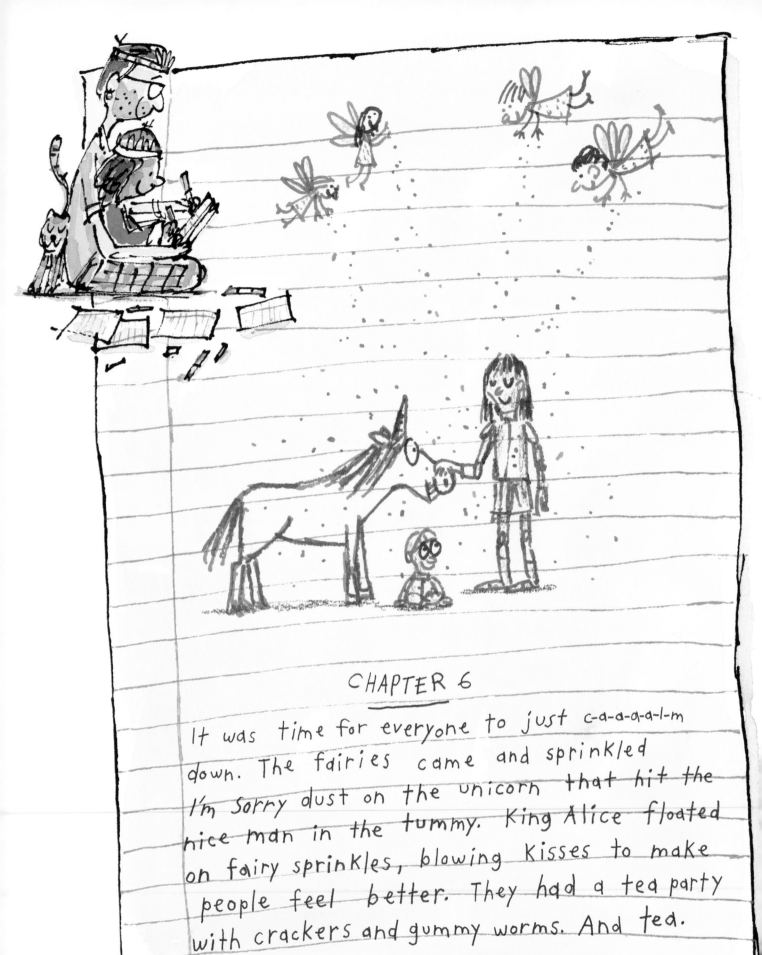

CHAPTER 6

It was time for everyone to just c-a-a-a-a-l-m down. The fairies came and sprinkled I'm Sorry dust on the unicorn that hit the nice man in the tummy. King Alice floated on fairy sprinkles, blowing kisses to make people feel better. They had a tea party with crackers and gummy worms. And tea.

CHAPTER 7

Then King Alice said to everybody, "Now, would you like to come for a sleepover at my house?"

The fairies sang "Happy Birthday" to help them fall asleep.

Captain Bellyfish said, "I'm still the toughest pirate on Earth!"

Y-a-a-a-a-a-w-n.

S-n-o-o-o-o-o-r-e.

THE END

"Y-a-a-a-a-w-n . . . I love snow days."

"Good night, Kitty Babies," said Alice. "Good night, Dad."
"Good night, sweetheart," said Dad.

"Idea! Tomorrow . . . ,"
Alice said . . .

"... let's make a **sequel**!!"

"Um . . . ," Dad said.